To Rumi . . . you have a special place in my heart!
—W. S.

To Krista, my not-so-secret valentine
—L.H.

two lions

Text copyright © 2022 by Wendi Silvano
Illustrations copyright © 2022 by Lee Harper
All rights reserved.

Published by Two Lions, New York
www.apub.com
Amazon, the Amazon logo, and Two Lions are trademarks of Amazon.com, Inc., or its affiliates.
ISBN-13: 9781542023665
ISBN-10: 1542023661

The illustrations were rendered in watercolor and pencil on Arches hot press watercolor paper.
Book design by Tanya Ross-Hughes
Printed in China
First Edition
10 9 8 7 6 5 4 3 2 1

Turkey's
Valentine Surprise

by
Wendi Silvano

illustrated by
Lee Harper

It was Valentine's Day, and all the animals
on Farmer Jake's farm were exchanging cards and treats.
Turkey pulled a card out of his valentine box.
His wattle wiggled with delight as he read the note.

"Oooooh . . . how **otter-ly** clever!" said Turkey.
"Valentines from a **secret** admirer are the most fun!"
He shook his tail feathers.

"I am going to make one for each of my pals. And I will deliver them in disguise so they stay secret!"
Turkey was determined to make valentines that were just as clever as the one he'd gotten. He just needed some inspiration.

Then he found it.

His costume wasn't bad. In fact, Turkey looked just like a cat . . . almost.
Inch by inch, he crept closer to Rooster's valentine box.

Just as he slipped the card inside,
Rooster flew down and grabbed it.

"I have a *feline* that you're not a cat . . .
you're Turkey!" said Rooster.
"But what a clever valentine!"

"Oh, gobble, gobble!" moaned Turkey. "I wanted it to be a secret surprise."

"Sorry," said Rooster.

"I know just the disguise to go with this. Horse won't notice an extra dog running around the farm."

His costume wasn't bad. In fact, Turkey looked just like a dog . . . almost.
Rooster threw a ball toward Horse's valentine box. "Fetch!" he crowed.

Turkey ran on all fours
the best he could.

"Woof! Woof!"

He dropped the valentine into Horse's box, grabbed the ball, and hid behind a bush to watch what would happen.

Horse read the card and peeked behind the bush. "You *mutt* as well come out, Turkey," he said. "I know it's you. But thanks for the nice valentine!"

"Oh, gobble, gobble," groaned Turkey. "I wanted it to be a secret surprise."

"Sorry," said Horse. "Maybe I can help you surprise someone else. Who's next?"

"Cow," said Turkey. "Just give me a minute to find another idea."

He made Cow's valentine.
"I know just the disguise to go with this.
Cow would think nothing of seeing a toad
hopping around the farm."

His costume wasn't bad.
In fact, Turkey looked just like a toad . . . almost.

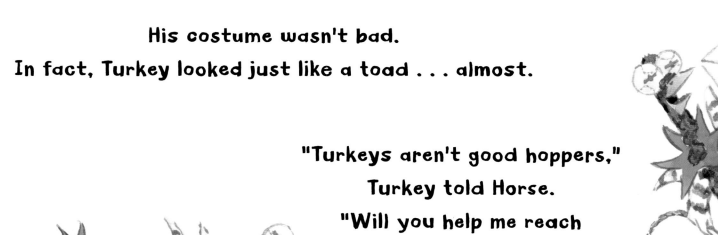

"Turkeys aren't good hoppers,"
Turkey told Horse.
"Will you help me reach
Cow's valentine box?"

Just as Turkey was about to put the card in Cow's box, Horse hit a bump.

Cow shook her head. "**Warts** up, Turkey? Why do you look like a toad?"

"Oh, gobble, gobble, gobble," wailed Turkey.
"I just wanted to give all my pals secret surprise valentine cards.
But they've all been ruined."

Cow read the card. "But it's still a wonderful valentine," she said.
"How about I help you deliver Sheep's and Pig's cards?
They're both in the barn."

"That would be *gobble, gobble great!*" said Turkey.
"An owl shouldn't have any trouble sneaking a valentine into their boxes.
They probably won't even look up."

His costume wasn't bad.
In fact, Turkey looked just like an owl . . . almost.

Cow and Turkey stealthily made their way up to the hayloft in the barn.
Cow held tight to the rope as she lowered Turkey down bit by bit.

Turkey swung left.

Turkey swung right.

He was almost there.

"Aaaaaachoo!"

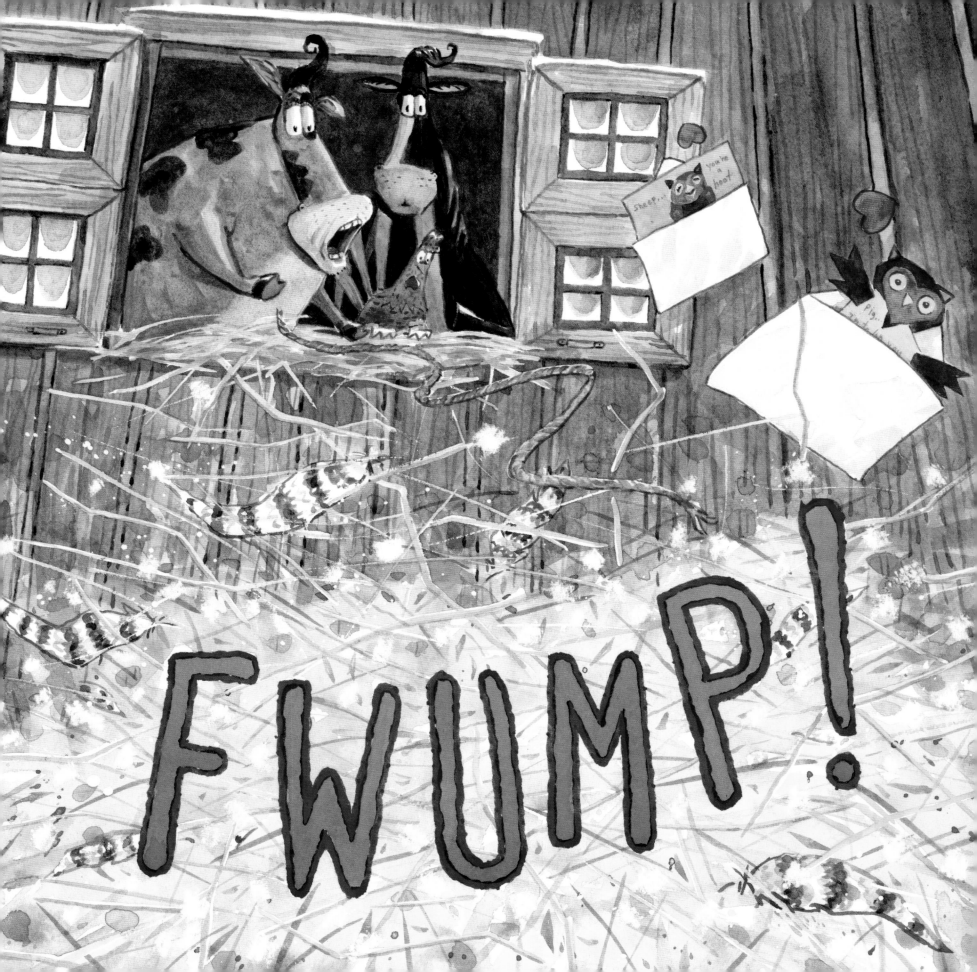

Sheep looked over at Pig. "Is it *owl* in my head, or did Turkey just fall from the sky?"

Pig picked up the fallen valentines and gave Sheep hers.
"Cool valentines, Turkey. Thank you!" said Pig.

Turkey sighed. "I *gobble, gobble, give up!*
I wanted you all to get surprise secret valentines because they're the most fun.
But you all found out they were from me."

"Your valentines were still great!" said Sheep.

"And so clever!" said Cow.

"We loved them!" said Pig.

"Us too!" said Rooster and Horse.

Turkey trudged over to his box and plopped down.
"Maybe next year I can surprise them."
He decided to distract himself from his disappointment
by reading his own valentines.

Then he saw a heart that
gave him one last idea!

"That's it!" screeched Turkey.
"I've got to hurry.
The Valentine's Dance starts
in just two hours!"

Turkey peeked into the barn. No one was there yet.

He delivered his secret surprise
and hustled away unseen.

At the dance, everyone was delighted with the delicious pizza.

Turkey couldn't keep from smiling.
"No one will ever know it was me!" he said.
"This is the most clever Valentine surprise ever!"